MALAIKA

VAN HEERLING

D1608041

www.vanheerlingbooks.com

Cover Design, Book Interior and Copy Editing
by The Book Khaleesi
www.thebookkhaleesi.com

THE STORY

A middle-aged man with the crushing weight of his American past seeks peace and a simpler life in rural Kenya. Armed with only his smokes and coffee, he discovers a friendship with the most unlikely of friends—a lioness he rightfully names Malaika, "Angel" in Swahili. But she is no ordinary lioness, nor is he an ordinary man. Between them they share a gift. But not all embrace their bond and some seek to sever it.

Discover this new world rich in human Truth and Sensibility.

PRAISE for MALAIKA

"An excellent piece of writing that I enjoyed immensely..."

"...it is a gift to relish and savor...a keeper to the nth degree."

"This is by far the best piece of literature, under full novel length, I have EVER read, and I cannot wait to read this author's next work."

ACKNOWLEDGEMENT

I would like to thank my mother for allowing me to become my father's son, and not faulting me for it. And to my wife, for navigating the countless storms I have caused.

For my father.

You missed so much.

TABLE of CONTENTS

"In the end, we are either loved or we are not. No matter what one has done, it is never too late to press the soles of one's feet back toward a path of rightness, of goodness, and of forgiveness."

~ VH ~

MALAIKA

(Ma-lie-ka)

The first time I saw her, I was dazed but recovering from hellish nightmares. Not sure if it was the scent of coffee lackadaisically meandering across the Serengeti that brought us to our serendipitous moment (do big cats drink coffee?), or if it was that she had told me she'd be here soon. I generally don't have conversations with animals—other than the human kind. I suppose, if the dialogue occurred in a dream, you aren't crazy, right?

As far as how I came to live just inside Kenya at the Tanzanian border overlooking the Serengeti, well, that is another lifetime dappled with hurt and a lost love elsewhere in the world—I won't bore you with the details. I wanted to get as far away from that pain as I could. The 'geti is about as distant as I could travel. Funny, no matter how far one has traveled, the past is just a moment. . . just a thought away.

I will not taint this story with that past. This is a story of a more recent past, of a friendship—the most important friendship I've ever had.

I live east of a village. I am the only white man for probably twenty miles or more. I suppose there could be a few around, or many in town, but I haven't seen any. This life can be hard to adapt to, especially when one is accustomed to the rote American life of excess for its own sake. Pressure. That is part of the reason why I left. No, that is a lie. It's not why I left, but I promised I wouldn't scar this story with my American past. There may be a trace of it betrayed here and there, but I will do my best to check such impulses.

Where was I? Oh, yes—life is slower here. Not in a dimwitted way, but in a take-a-deep-breath-and-*live* kind of way. Speaking of breaths, I promised that I wouldn't start smoking again. But that was in my old life. I made a lot of promises then; this is now. I don't smoke processed cigarettes—Western market contraband. No, my good friend Abasi is a tobacco farmer. Did I say he's a good friend? He's a great friend; genuine, forthright, and not afraid to smack the hell out of you when you need it or deserve it. More often than not, I am the latter. Who would have known I'd have to travel halfway around the world to find a friend that wasn't a sycophant. One of his virtues is that he doesn't know the meaning of the word.

I teach Absko, his son, English in exchange for fresh tobacco, among other things. Truth told, I'd do it for free. He knows this. Sometimes I work the fields with him. Wielding a machete and tying bundles have been unbearably taxing at times. Although I have tried not to let it show on my face, everyone knows—I'm not fooling anyone. One could say I'm paying for my deep-seated American complacency, I suppose.

I must make one point very clear: I am not "anti-American way." Far from it. This is, like I said, just a different way of life. It is nothing here to slaughter your own food, or dig your own latrine, or hear of children starving to death, despite Doctors Without Borders. Unsheltered is what I mean. Far from texting and live streaming with friends.

I will one day go back. Maybe.

CHAPTER ONE

The weight of my waking body sagged as my hand dangled off the beaten plastic armrest. My fingertips stuck to the lip of an American coffee cup. Mostly because of the moisture in my palm, rather than my grip. My God, she was quiet. Had I been her culinary desire, I definitely would have been it. For some reason, the nostalgic disco beats of the seventies circled the air ducts of my mind. In hindsight, perhaps this was a coping mechanism. It seemed I had been through more in the last couple years than I cared to think about.

My other hand gingerly held a loosely rolled cigarette—in the early mornings I am not as motivated as most of the workforce, no doubt readying themselves for their day's toil.

I rolled the tobacco up to my lip, my eyelids shut to the cresting sun over Kenyan mountains. The fiery smoke warmed my throat from the morning chill. This African tobacco chars more tender throats, but my once-virginal uvula and esophagus had toughened up long ago. The fire these days simply continued to callous the linings of my ever-embattled breathing pipe. It's an acquired taste. It is earned, I suppose. An argument for my ex-wife? Perhaps.

It was to be a very clear day. January usually is, and hot of course. But this goes without saying—I wasn't used to the opposite seasons yet. The only ones who complain about the heat are foreigners, so I complain—God, do I complain.

I readjusted my back for a moment, lifting the slipping cup of joe to my mouth, and then lowering it back to its roosting spot a foot or so off the ground, dangling from my fingertips.

She was quiet. When you live in the wild and your hand is pushed into the air by what can only be bad, you notice. You notice real fast. I wasn't sure if I had leapt from the foldout chair when I heard the guttural sniff or if I was already standing. This was a beast. At least three hundred pounds—a big cat. She paid little attention to me at first. Sniffing the spilt coffee as it contoured to the cracked earth. Pawing it, she sniffed and lapped up what she could find. Then, licking her chops, she raised her head squarely at me. The sun looming over the mountains reflected in her eyes. Her body language was uninhibited, relaxed even, but those eyes—burned fierce.

Swiftly I realized that neither one of us was moving. Not good. I had frozen five feet away from her with my cigarette hand extended toward her as if the fiery cherry were a shield. I didn't want to be the first to move. Then, I remembered the "deer in the headlights" syndrome, and thought—shit, move your ass! Just as I was about to shift my body weight backward, her eyes flickered toward my intended route. Smart. They're not known as killing machines because they were guessers.

Lions never hunt alone . . . I was a goner for sure. Knowing this could be the end, I figured I better take another drag. When Abasi finds what was left of me, he'd discover the last remnants of his sweet, sweet tobacco. I gently pulled my cherry shield back to my lips. I wasn't dead yet or being dragged into the jungle. Good sign. So I sucked. It was the best smoke I'd ever had. Still not dead. Even better. I exhaled quietly as the smoke billowed from my mouth. She tilted her head up toward the expanding cloud of "Kenyan's Best," and, sniffing the air, her nostrils flared. She shook her head and huffed from the foreign and relatively concentrated dose.

Not that I wanted to see my disembowelment chasing me up, I did look, albeit slowly, to my right and my left. No other interested visitors that I could see. I wasn't about to turn my back on this feline. Although I was sure I'd be dead in less than five minutes, I gazed toward the house. It was wide open, both doors and all three windows. Even if I could manage to get inside, she'd be on my heels or through a window before I could grab and cock my shotgun. I'd be wrestling a full-grown lion in a four hundred square foot sand brick hut. That is, if I could even make it through the door.

She never took her eyes from me as she sniffed the air again. I billowed out yet another tobacco cloud. She sniffed the air a third time, but didn't recoil from the smoke. Placing one paw toward me, her eyes continued to deadlock on mine but they now lacked the fierceness of before. She sniffed the air again, I puffed again, and she took another step toward me. Too close. I panicked and feebly pushed the cigarette from my hand. It landed just in front of her fuchsia and ebony-edged nostrils. I took two steps back. She noticed, but preoccupied herself with my token expression of "please-don't-eat-me." Huddling in front of the smoldering tobacco, hunched down, she investigated the curious object.

"Careful. It's h—" Her tongue peeled from her massive mouth and pressed against the ember. She yelped loudly and hissed, bouncing backward. "—ot," I finished. She shook her head angrily in my direction, as if to say, "How about a little warning next time?"

"I tried to tell you but—" That was when I realized I was talking to a lion. I'm not sure why, but she didn't eat me. Her composure came back somewhat as she began to cautiously pull her body forward. She was proud. Head high, shoulders and back straight. Really just a marvelous creature. The muddled russet coat was truly brilliant to behold, especially so close up.

I held my hand out palm up because I'm an idiot, I know... but it seemed like the proper thing to do at the time. I was right. She tentatively pressed the crown of her head against my knuckles. I wasn't ready for the sheer power. She rubbed her body against my pant leg, nearly knocking me to the ground. I pressed my hand against her fur. It was surprisingly soft, but thick and rugged—if it is possible to be both at the same time. She circled me two times. I didn't move much. Then, she treaded her footsteps back to my chair, sniffed at the coffee-sodden ground again, and trotted back into the jungle.

I felt ashamed about wanting to take her down. Although I'm sure it crossed her mind once or twice. So maybe we were even.

CHAPTER TWO

`

B y the time Absko showed up, it was late morning, coming upon noon. He was a strong boy. His body well into the advanced stage of puberty; that awkward period when you're not sure which or what was growing. He approached shirtless. It wasn't hot for him and truth be told, vanity was setting in these days. His upper body could now bear two heavy bundles of tobacco with little effort.

My door was always open, more or less. It wasn't like I had a dead bolt or anything, or even a lock. Anyone coming out this far would be intending to see me, and I haven't as of yet, made any enemies that I knew of.

The screen door yielded its familiar whine as the coiled metal spring flexed—subsequently slapping the door shut as Absko entered. He set his books on a small table accompanying a worn book of Emerson, headed for the icebox, and popped open an A&W. I had just gotten them. My favorite.

"Absko," I said, "what did you learn today?"

"At school or in life?" he replied, anticipating my answer.

"In life, my boy, in life!" This was routine talk between us; somehow, it hadn't run its lot yet.

"I learned today that I could lie to my father and get away with it." He waited, testing me to see if I'd approve or rebuke such a discovery.

"Hmm, I see. Yes, very good—learning the art of

deception. However, don't be surprised if that comes back to haunt you one day. Especially if your father never finds out."

"Don't you want to know what it is about?"

"And there it starts . . . nope, Absko, I most definitely do not want to know about it. That is yours alone."

"What 'starts'?" he questioned.

"You'll find out soon enough. I'll give you a hint, though. Deception is a wicked instrument, and when used against the ones we love . . . well, like I said, you'll one day learn a new lesson."

"Are you going to tell him?"

"No, Absko, but you might."

He took a sip of root beer as he brooded over this. As a bright boy, I knew he basically understood my warning, but the full circle of understanding wouldn't hit him until life pressed it on him.

"Nah, I don't think he needs to know, not about this one."

I pulled a root beer for myself and traded a wry smile with him. Abasi was my best friend, but only if it were dire enough would I break the confidence I had earned from his son. I had a feeling Absko's deceit in this case was child's play (I was wrong).

I grabbed my tobacco pouch and some papers and headed to my dilapidated but trusty chair just out front. Absko followed silently, grabbing his yellow, faded foldout, and set up next to mine.

"So have *you* learned anything today?" he asked.

"Hmm, yes. I learned I might not be as safe out here as I thought I would be."

Absko raised his head from the back of his chair, a bit frightened. I had never spoken of such things. He waited for me to continue.

"I was visited by a lioness, 'bout three hundred pounds."

"Ha! OK, funny, you got me. You'd have been shredded." When I didn't reciprocate his playfulness, it sunk in. "A lioness? Are you serious?"

"Yep, gorgeous too. Check the paw prints at your feet." He did, his eyes wide open. "She knocked my coffee—"

"You didn't shoot it?"

"Oh no, first of all, I would have been done for had she so desired. Plus, the gun was in the house. But I have to tell you, she looked right at me. It was almost like she just came by to say hello."

"How many were there?

"Just her."

"No, that is what she wanted you to see. When they hunt, there would have easily been five or six stalking you."

"She wasn't hunting," I said plainly.

"How do you know?"

"Well, Absko, I'm talking to you, aren't I?"

He fell quiet. He didn't like what I was saying. No one was a friend of the felines. Most of the time the cats were killed on sight if they entered the villages. Most probably knew not to enter, and the ones that didn't know usually learned with their lives. Absko's cousin was killed by one of them. An all-out hunt was summarily dispatched against the nearest pride. Perhaps the saddest thing besides the loss of his cousin was that no one was sure if the particular pride they slaughtered was the offending family. No matter, of course, to men of revenge and reckoning.

"Well, I don't like it. Have you told my dad?"

"You're the first person I have seen today. When you see him, ask him to bring some of the passion fruit and bobby beans he had last week. I'm all out."

"No problem. You should lock your door tonight."

"Don't have a lock. I'll be all right. Like I said, it was just the one. Hey, Absko, let's keep this between us for the time being."

"Sure. I learned another thing today."

"Yeah? What's that?"

"I think I'm going to need a new English teacher," he said, straight-faced.

"Well, it wouldn't be the first time I've been dominated by a pussy," I retorted. It was immature I know, but I knew it'd get a rise out of a sixteen-year-old. "Cheers," I chuckled, as we clanked tin cans together and drank the sweet nectar they call the "Beer of Root."

CHAPTER THREE

I slept fully, unlike most nights. And unlike most nights, I dreamed. I preferred nothingness while sleeping in place of the nightmares, of course. But up until last night, I had nearly forgotten the pleasures of dreams without horrifying qualities. She came back to me. We sat next to each other and watched the sunrise. I put my hand on her back and petted her golden coat—speckled with a rusty brown and slivers of ebony. And for some reason, to my right lay my wife on her own foldout chair. She was young like when we first met, sunbathing, rubbing oil on her arms and neck. Smiling at me like nothing had happened. She was happy. Then I woke up. The sun would show soon.

As before, I held my coffee at the tips of my fingers. I half-hoped, crazy as it might seem, that she would come back and that the dream would be more than a random projection of my own desires. Sipping my coffee, I trembled at the thought of her, the cat, coming back—not my wife. Two different creatures altogether. The cat could disembowel me, after all— well, now that I think of it, the ex could, too.

The foldout chair creaked and twanged under my weight.

The peeking sun was just beginning to caress the mountaintops. I took another sip as the golden light splashed across my face. If not for the overpowering taste of the coffee, I could have smelled this light. I looked to my right and saw not a sun-tanning twenty-five-year-old other half, but an empty meadow, flush with wild grasses, the tips of which were painted by the light—kissing them with auburn and blond hues.

To my left was a cat staring into the rising sun with such concentration, I thought she might be praying to a light god. Perhaps, if I had any good sense, I would have recreated the same spectacle as yesterday: the dramatic leap from the thrifty foldout with my arms pressed forward while hiding behind the cherry glow of my loosely rolled cigarette. For starters, I don't have any sense, and also, I had yet to prep a smoke. Instead, I sat. I sat with my legs stretched across the length of the plastic chair, my boney kneecaps exposed to a potential mauling.

Who am I kidding? My whole body could be a chew toy to her. I raised my coffee to my bottom lip. The steam effervesced against my face as I swallowed. She had a glint of green within her eyes that I hadn't noticed before. I noticed this after the sound of my sip pulled her from her prayer to the sun god. She was unpretentious as she stared directly into my eyes. I wasn't sure what to do, so I smiled gently, making sure not to expose my teeth just in case it be construed as universal aggression. Her attention did not go to my mouth, but rather stayed with my eyes. I swear my smile was reciprocated, as she then maneuvered her head back to the shimmering light splintering over the mountains.

Déjà vu struck me as I turned my gaze to the mountains as well. This was my dream. I looked to my right, again expecting to see my wife, but of course, she wasn't there. My friend turned to me again, seemingly acknowledging my thought. Slowly I reached for my tin full of tobacco and papers. My lioness friend was not threatened by me. And to my surprise, my guard had been slipping away. She pouted her nose in the air toward the tin just as she'd done before when she smelled the tobacco smoke the first time.

"Oh, you remember this, don't you?" I said, breaking the silence. My voice was thick. As I rolled a cigarette, she studied my process. Her eyes then lifted to my face as I lit it. A puff of white smoke expelled from me. Her nostrils flared delightfully as she moved closer, bumping the arm of the chair. I nearly toppled over. I let her smell it as I set it in front of her nose, my hand mere inches from her pink-stained mouth. Intrigued by this smell, she rolled her tongue out to lap it. Retracting my hand as fast as I could, narrowly missing the rasp that was her tongue, I said, "No, hot!"

Her head tilted forward as she contemplated my sounds.

She snorted annoyingly and sat back down on her haunches. I think she remembered the burning of her tongue on the previous ember. I took another drag and exhaled. She enjoyed it vicariously through me as the smell permeated the air around us. Then, because I'm stupid, remember, I placed my hand on her back. She allowed me to pet her a bit, and then she got up and began her return to the meadow. I didn't intend to follow her, but she stopped and waited for me. This was unfamiliar territory. The dream had come to fruition for the most part. She took me fifty yards from the perimeter of my property, further into the meadow. This was apparently the point where Tanzania and the actual Serengeti began. As far as I was concerned, it was all 'geti to me. Beyond the perimeter was a shallow valley hidden by a rim of trees and bush. Beyond that point, I no longer felt safe. When first settling in, I walked most of the area around my home. As I approached this area, I felt—tracked. From that point on I learned to stay on the trails that led to the village and water supply.

Standing next to me, her back at my waist, I soon realized why she stopped. At the tree line sat three cold-faced lions. A male in the middle and two lionesses. To say they were jovial to see us would be a funny twist of truth. Soon, my friend mirrored their unfriendly posturing. I stood there like an oaf.

No wonder I felt like I was being tracked when I had

journeyed this way. For all intents and purposes, I probably was. But this time, this moment, was immeasurably worse. Was I breakfast? Had I been betrayed by my new friend? A tremor of terror struck me. She must have figured out what I was thinking because she flanked my leg and nuzzled my hand with her head. I felt better, but not confident I was going to walk away safe. Not a flinch from the audience of three. Her actions toward me had distilled their disapproval into more of a fury, and then they glowered.

Submissively, she bowed her head, tucking her tail in close to her legs as she walked the fifty yards to her—guardians? I raised my hand as she tentatively looked back at me before disappearing through the trees and down into the ravine. The females had followed her. As for me, the king of beasts stood squared to me not fifty yards from my boney knees. My gnawable, boney knees. He took one step forward. His entire coat shook as he stepped into a definite and calculated pose. No need for a lion-to-human translation. He did not scan the land around me. He did not flinch. His address was to me. A gentle breeze wisped through the king's mane. As if made of stone dressed with russet fur, he did not budge. Rock-solid. His chin rose and nostrils flared, just like my friend. But his was a malevolent gesture. He'd deciphered my scent. A scent he wouldn't soon forget. The roar that now came from his mouth was more of a guttural rebuke. I was an annoyance to him. Then, although moderated, the second roar seemed to concentrate within my inner ear and did not penetrate much further than the meadow. This warning was for me alone, not for the surrounding African audience. It was acute, painful.

Unknown to me, until I felt the warmth percolating through the fabric of my drawers, a splash of fright had wetted my leg. I was able to halt it, but couldn't make any promises if another step was taken. His scruff was pinkish with blood, similar to my visitor. Even if he may have already eaten, it didn't mean he wouldn't still feast upon the problem at hand. His belly was capacious, no doubt from several large meals in his lifetime. I'm sure half a zebra and an unclean washed-up schmuck could fit just fine, albeit snugly. On the other hand, he could simply maul me just to prove a point. Either way, I was at his mercy. Couldn't run to the house, and even if I could, I doubted the walls could hold a four-hundred-pound cat from a determined entrance.

Calculatingly, his shoulders commandeered his body back to the tree line, his man-lion parts swaggering from side to side. Then he was gone.

Soaking in my surroundings, I felt the high grass at my fingertips and heard White-tailed Swallows singing their songs. Up to this point, I had not known they were cheerfully crooning to their mates while my life, as seemingly inconsequential as it was, hung in the balance. Had the now-absentee king decided to tear me limb from limb, these cheery birds of the Serengeti might have improvised a lovely melody while I wailed and pleaded for my existence.

And there, two hundred yards from my own home, I peed myself. I peed myself uncontrollably.

CHAPTER FOUR

W eeks had passed, and I had many encounters with the lioness. For this, I knew I would have to answer to my dear friend sooner or later. Abasi, as I had said before, is an honorable man. Judging by his scarred chest and the razor-thin white marble flesh under his left eye—a keepsake from a knife fight from decades past still lingering—one would think he was a man of ill intentions. But these imperfections hid kindness.

Abasi's body absorbed the heat of the midafternoon as he walked shirtless toward my desolate hut. He was stronger than his son, of course, still in his prime, if a bit on the waning side. Dangling from his mouth lurched a long piece of wild grass. Within the grasp of his rough, thick-skinned hands hung two bags filled with fresh vegetables and fruit.

I had retreated to the porch, which consisted of sheet metal riveted to the roof and two long stakes on either end. In the middle the metal bowed generously, which was helpful during the rains. Water concentrated into one spot allowed me to shower if desired, without having to commingle with the community at the lake. But this luxury was seldom.

I thanked my friend as I took the produce, setting it just inside the door. As he sat beside me, he seemed troubled. Not in an alarming way; just in a way that a friend knows. I passed an ale, hoping it would help put him at ease.

After a sip he surveyed the meadow and sighed as he turned to me. "Tell me, friend, what is this I hear in the tobacco fields, the market, and from my own son?"

"Well, Abasi, being that I don't usually attend social gatherings within the tobacco fields, or the market, and well, I haven't enjoyed your hospitality in weeks, you tell me. What is it that you hear?"

Abasi stared at his bare feet, dry and cracked, as he gently smiled at his stubborn American friend's coy disposition.

"Have I shared about the time Sherri and I went on a picnic?"

"I can't say that you have."

"Absko was but a bump within his mother's belly. She was so beautiful this day. Her beauty shined each day she walked this earth, but this day in particular."

I could tell Abasi could see her clearly as he continued with his story. It pained me because I knew that deep within him he still hurt tremendously from his loss, even though sixteen years had passed.

"I helped her down a ravine and soon we came upon a lovely grassy knoll under a Strangler Fig tree, where adjacent to our setting I did pluck the most perfect bloom from a Sausage tree for her to set in her hair." His lips found another sip of the ale. "We were enjoying berries from her mother's garden. I can still see her smile."

Abasi paused a moment. His chapped lips receded from his teeth, exposing them to the day. His brow furrowed, but then his countenance turned repentant and remorseful. "I was rubbing her belly and had my ear to her when I felt a shudder in her body. Her palm urgently pounded my back; her jovial enchantment drained away and was replaced by terror. As I gazed upon her delicate face, it was pale and fearful. Then I heard that wicked deep growl that can only be the supreme of hunters. It was the matriarch and her adolescents that numbered two. Had I reacted in haste, we would surely have been finished. I know this to be true. They were hungry indeed.

"The matriarch was perhaps brazen in her training of her young. Instead of pouncing when we were unaware, it almost seemed that she wanted us to witness our demise. To this day, I do not know why they had not encountered us by surprise. I do not dwell on this, but I am thankful for that oversight." He gripped the ale bottle with both palms as he recalled his story, his upper body trembling just the faintest bit as he continued. "You know the correct outcome of this story in part as you have seen some of my scarred body."

He raised his left leg and showed me his inner thigh, which had been mutilated, only to heal in a contorted condition. "This was the most devastating injury of that encounter, I am happy to say in retrospect, for it could have been many times worse had I not had the rifle at my side." His fingers delicately massaged the once torn flesh as he looked at me.

"As she approached, haste now came upon me and I reached for my weapon. The round was absent from the chamber, and the time it took to cock the weapon was the moment she pounced upon me. Being young, I was quick to my feet but wasn't fast enough to aim the rifle at her. Besides, she was now too close. I can still feel her breath and sheer strength as she sprung forward. I came down hard and fast against her crown with the butt of the rifle. A shot fired into the blue; had the sky been made of glass, the shot would have splintered it. The anguish and fear I felt pumped through my veins.

"The youths, after the crack of the shot, did not approach us, but the matron, though dazed from the blow, was far from retreating as her jaws latched on to my leg as you can see here." He pointed to a healed puncture mark. "I fell to the ground and knew that I was going to die this day. This thought did not trouble me as much as the regret I felt for Sherri. For she would soon meet a similar plight. With the lioness's bite as I said, I had fallen and with that I lost grip of the weapon. I reached for the lion's face and feebly poked and prodded for her eyes, but she was simply too overwhelming. My blows were formidable had they landed against another man's body, but at best for this cat, they were glancing, if only a feeble distraction to her training.

"I heard another crack of the rifle against the blue sky and a vibration through my nemesis. Then another and another. Sherri, with her pregnant belly, had cocked and laid three shots into the flank of the matriarch. The cat released her grip. The determination of the hunt faded within her eyes as she gazed into mine not half an arm's length away. Slowly, she hobbled away from us.

"Sherri cocked the rifle again as I lay bleeding. With the beast in her crosshairs, she fired again but missed as the hunters retreated into a thick of trees. I raised my hand, asking her to let them be. It was done. I knew the lioness was abiding by nature's law and that her impulse to hunt us was my fault, because I was unaware of my place. To her, we were fair game."

I pondered this theory for a moment as I continued to listen.

"Sherri was weeping as she set the rifle at my side. Her one hand groped me for injuries not yet seen while she plunged the other hand into my inner thigh wrapped with her cloth napkin. I winced because of the pain, of course, but mostly because of the fear within her eyes as she feverishly managed me. She ripped off my shirt and secured it around my hemorrhaging thigh.

"Debris was strewn about us from the Strangler Fig and shortly she procured a decent crutch that we may start our trek back to the village. You know the rest of the story as I am sitting here." He was somber, collected in his thoughts as he finished his ale. I handed him another, and he gladly accepted.

"I have two regrets that are separate from the point I must impart to you today. I failed her that day by not protecting her. I feel deep shame that I was not strong enough to protect her."

"Yes, but—" I interrupted, attempting to highlight his considerable contributions that day. He raised his hand to me, not interested in my justifications to make him feel more at ease.

"And the other," he continued, "is the day Absko was born. This, of course, as I have told you in the past, was the day Sherri left this world. In her battle of birth, I could not help her. I watched her die as the doctor feebly attended to her. These are two regrets I have and must live with."

"Yes, but Abasi, how can you blame yourself for something that was fated, as your people have said?"

"I do not expect you to understand. This is not why I have told you what I have today. The reason for my story is we have a place in life. We belong to a system, and every piece has its place. That day, this lioness was doing as she was supposed to—hunt. As we did as we were supposed to, which was defend what is ours. But, my friend, what I hear in my village I do not like, this talk about a man who intermingles with a wild cat. The one that hand-feeds and pets it like it's a mere house cat. This is not your place. It will end badly. For you are tempting a fate for which I lived just barely, as you can see from my wounds."

He was quiet for some time.

"Abasi, hand-fed? No, I have not done any such thing." Then I thought about her licking the tobacco. Maybe Absko construed this as hand-feeding. "You don't know what has transpired." I continued, "You don't know what I have experienced. We met in a dream, we shared your tobacco."

"So it is true what I have heard. They say you have the lion's tongue."

I laughed gently, surmising that Absko's tight lips must have loosened.

"What do you suppose you will gain from this friendship?" he asked defensively.

"Nothing," I said. "You do not know the whole truth. You are my dearest friend but you've allowed yourself to be strayed by your own demons and hearsay."

He did not appreciate my blunt honesty. His chest plumed, eager for verbal retaliation, but then he simmered, perhaps remembering my wisdom in past conversations.

"Then, my American friend, please enlighten me as to why I am wrong and how it is that you will not be killed?"

"I never said I would not be killed. That, I cannot promise. If she had the desire, I would have been lion waste weeks ago. She comes to me a few minutes before daybreak. We enjoy your tobacco, and sometimes a saucer of coconut milk. I may pour some ale in a dish. We wrestle for a time, if desired, and then nap." I gestured toward my hut.

"You allow this animal in your home?" he asked intently.

"Sure, not that I really have a choice in the matter. I huddle up in my bed, and she naps on the floor. She is self-reliant. She will not let me brush the knots from her coat, on the rare occasion that there are knots, nor will she take a blanket during a chilly night."

Abasi scoffed at my ignorance. "Tell me about this dreaming you have."

"Not much to tell. I dream vividly now. My nightmares are all but gone. She and I speak to one another."

"Like English-speak," he laughed deridingly.

"No, not like English-speak. It is more of a conceptual communication. Thought transference. Somehow I am able to translate her concepts into a language I understand. And she can do the same. Abasi, I don't expect you to understand. Frankly, I don't totally understand it myself. It's more than what I am saying, but I can't quite communicate it, I guess, because I am trying to describe the communicative properties of one world to another, when the properties are entirely different."

"Absko *was* right," he said mockingly.

"What?"

"He said that he was going to need a new English teacher soon." He smiled.

"Hmm, yes, maybe. Well, we both know I haven't been his teacher for a while now. Mostly we just bounce philosophy off each other's heads. Besides, the schoolhouse seems to be doing a far better job than I could. By the way, so much for him keeping my secret, huh?"

"He's just concerned. He thinks very highly of his mysterious American friend that has fled his own country in search of simplicity. Which I find ironic in that the complication you so desire to avoid is catching you up and you have yet to recognize this." I knew there was truth to what he was saying, but at the time, I did not want to listen. "I am hurt that you did not come to me about your new friendship," he said as he wiped droplets off his sweating ale.

"Had I, what would you have told me?"

"I would have said that you are mad and would have had you purged of this demon by the shaman." We both laughed.

Neither of us held much stock in such things.

"And now?" I inquired.

"Well, now it is too late for you. No purge will rid you of this displaced friendship."

"I see."

"Well, I have made my peace and have said what I had intended." He stood, stretching his arms above him, still clasping the ale. With a healthy sigh, he admonished, "The council members have asked that I give you a formal warning about your arrangement. As you well know, the beasts are not allowed in the village, and if she follows you there, she will be killed. I tell you this not to hurt you, but so that you may make arrangements so this does not occur. There have been too many casualties in the past to allow you exception."

I held my drink in salute to him. "Abasi," I said as he walked away, "she is the most gentle soul I have ever come to be acquainted with. I daresay she may be an angel."

He turned to me squarely and endearingly said, "*Malaika.*"

"What's that?" I asked.

"It is Swahili for angel."

"Angel?" I pondered. "I like that very much."

"But when she has your neck between her fangs, will she be an angel or a demon unveiled?"

"Again you don't understand, I—"

"Then tell me. Why risk your life? Incredible dreams or not." He returned and sat back down.

"I can't let this go. Can't let this be taken away. It is all I have left. My wife—gone. I don't get to see my children. I'm a man without a home."

Abasi's plump lips tightened in amusement as he held his tongue.

"It seems you have something to say," I said, slightly offended.

"It appears that African loss is quite different than American loss."

"How so?" I inquired critically, fuming internally about the injustices of my life.

"Well, my friend, if I may be blunt, all this time you have talked about how *you* walked away from your American life. How *you* walked away from your wife. And the reasons you have put forth to me about why and how your children would be better if *you* left. You may see your wife and children at any time, however. They are only a sea away. This is the American loss I speak of. Now, African loss—this *is* the 'taken' you speak of so willingly. With the loss I speak of—it is more than a mere ocean I must cross. For if it were, I surely wouldn't be here speaking to a crazy American man drowning in his make-believe sorrows. I would be five hundred miles into the ocean toward my wife—swimming without missing a stroke, and I would not stop until I had her back in my arms. But what I speak of is fairy tales. In this life, what I speak of will never be. Not to mention I have lost many of my friends and family to famine and disease. But you, you have what has been 'taken' from you still warm within your breast, but you are too righteous to *see* what is plain for all to see."

He was right, though I didn't tell him so. I know now that it hurt him to be so blunt with me.

He pressed his rough palm against my shoulder compassionately, almost as if in apology.

"And it is not true," he continued "that you have lost everything. I am here. You have me."

I only gazed forward and nodded reluctantly. He shrugged as he turned from me and headed back to the tobacco fields.

CHAPTER FIVE

T he next evening I stood in the meadow, a seed of flickering contempt curdling in my stomach. As Malaika met The Three at the edge of the meadow, the patriarch butted his crown against hers, making a sound like two coconuts cracking against each other. The two females then hissed her into submission. It appeared like she was receiving the same "greeting" from her world as I was from mine. The last few times I had met with The Three were without incident. Meaning, they paid little attention to me. Thus, I didn't have the urge to pee myself. Abasi may have been right. Maybe we were tempting fate. As they disappeared down the ravine, I turned, but I could still hear their guttural snarls. I wished she had a compassionate friend such as I had in Abasi.

Days later, I found myself walking at the edges of the village. It had been a while since I had left my relatively isolated home. Near midday, I was maybe one hundred yards from the edges of the tobacco fields, and although I could not make out their faces, I knew the village folk recognized me when most stopped and turned toward me with their machetes in hand.

"Man with the lion's tongue," I scoffed endearingly. It wasn't a moment later that my feet bumped violently over my head from a leveling head-butt to the back of my thighs. As I lay there staring into the African blue sky, she wrestled playfully, pouncing around me. When I caught my breath, I grabbed her around the tuft of her neck and roared lightheartedly. I could hear some of the field workers laughing hysterically at the spectacle. She really was a hunter. I had no warning. However, my jubilation quickly drained as I noticed not all were amused. In fact, most were grasping their weapons. She read my fear as she stared into my eyes. I picked myself up and quickly walked back toward my "segregated" rental. She stayed at my side, and I petted her occasionally as we walked. All the while I thought about what Abasi said—Malaika would never be accepted in the village.

It wasn't long after I got home that Absko came over and began wrestling with Malaika. He had really warmed to her, and she to him. Occasionally, I would hear him squeal when her mouth came down a little harder than he would have liked.

"You should put a leash on her and parade her all around," he said.

"She is not mine to cage." I could have snarled at such a preposterous proposition, but I didn't.

CHAPTER SIX

That evening I walked with her to the edge of the meadow. The Three waited for us as before. This time was different as they sat on their haunches. The king raised himself upon seeing us. Although I was fifty yards away from him, it felt like a mere fifty inches. I was unwelcome, and he made this clear. Malaika passed me and within moments, passed her pride leader and met with the matriarchs. She turned toward me—perhaps indicating that we would meet again soon, then retreated.

"You know where you can find me," I whispered.

I don't remember lying long in my bed. When my head hit the pillow, I was out.

When the morning sun snuck over the mountains, I sat in my chair and waited for her. Drinking my coffee, I preempted a saucer of coconut milk for my soon-to-be guest.

Soon, I heard her lapping the milk, and I felt proud I had such a friend. With milk dripping from her chin, she radiated "good morning" in her eyes. I, admittedly, was giddy this crisp morning, for I had arranged a treat beyond anything I had supplied before. I reached into a cooler at my side. Her expression was of curiosity, but in hindsight, I figured she was being polite. With a lion-equipped-nose, it couldn't have been much of a surprise. I lifted wet butcher paper swamped with blood. As I opened it, I set it in front of her. Absko had provided me with a fresh cut of beef. Or at least I thought it was beef.

Malaika flared her nostrils over it, then turned to me with a glint in her eyes. Respectfully, she refused.

"Not *fresh* enough for you?" I asked. Exactly the case. Later, I found out that the kill was half of the meal, and that handouts were below her. I was forgiven for my cultural ignorance.

⌘ ⌘

A couple of weeks later, Absko peered his head into my room with a young lady on his arm. She was timid to her new surroundings and held him tightly. Her youth enhanced her remarkable beauty.

"This is Sanura."

Pulling my glasses from my face, I placed Ralph Waldo on the makeshift table, welcomed them, introduced myself, and offered them root beers.

"Absko, I assume this lovely young lady is your secret." They both shied against each other. He nodded, smiling, as she pressed her cheek against his shoulder, trying to hide her face. "Oh, my boy, what I would give if I could bottle what you two are feeling. That's wonderful, just wonderful."

"I'm sorry that I didn't ask first if I could bring a guest. I know how you like your privacy."

"Nonsense," I replied quickly. "Okay, you are right-on, but I am very willing to make an exception. I haven't seen your father in days, and frankly, it is nice to see you and a new face. So, Sanura, what is the meaning of such a beautiful name?"

She smiled as her gaze fell to the floor. "It means young cat."

"Is that right? Well, I'm sure your friend here has told you about a friend of mine."

"Yes, he has. The entire town knows about you and your friend."

"Yep, I have heard that as well. I wish they didn't know. If you stick around, she may come by in the evening. You feel like hanging around awhile?"

"I was hoping you'd ask that," she said as she looked up to Absko. Gently, he smiled and pressed his lips to her forehead.

"Oh, young love, how I wish I could bottle it. I'm jealous of you, young friend. So very jealous," I said, as we made our way out to the porch and sat, watching the daylight bleed away.

After a few hours of banter and a couple thousand points of rummy, Malaika entered our camp, seemingly unsurprised by our new guest. Sanura became wide-eyed, immediately frightened. Absko assured her everything was fine. Both slowly stood while I stayed in my chair. She bumped her head into my hovering palm as she passed me.

"Malaika," I said proudly, "I would like you to meet Sanura, or young cat." She walked toward the kids and held her gaze upon this new visitor. She flared her nostrils, smelling what was there to be sniffed. Sanura was visibly scared as Malaika walked toward her side and ever-so-slightly brushed her body against Sanura's upper thigh and waist. Then the cat bumped Absko with a robust head bump against his backside, but made sure not to jostle Sanura too much. Absko belted out a hardy laugh as they resumed their last wrestling match.

Sanura sat back down and watched in awe, this humongous beast vigorously rough-housing with her sweetheart.

"Sanura, tell me how you met such a hopelessly in love boy as that one right there."

She was beginning to open up. Hours of rummy and laughs and root beers will do that.

"We met when we were just children, but recently, we started noticing each other."

"I've got news for you—you're still children."

"You know what I mean."

"I suppose I do."

"I was hoping you could do me a favor."

"Depends on what that is, darling."

"It's kind of dumb, but I was hoping you could tell me what American name would fit me."

"Why would you want an American name?" Absko grunted, as he tried to lift Malaika, but was quickly countered as she pressed her fangs against his thigh. She wasn't about to be lifted. With each inch raised, she pressed harder against his thigh, and soon, he realized that it wasn't to be. Sanura and I practically fell down with laughter.

After Sanura regained her composure, she said, "Because one day, I want to live in America."

I realized before she said it that this was the reason. It saddened me, but I understood. I could fault her, but I was doing the same thing, in a way.

"I see. Well, let me size you up so I can figure out an acceptable 'American' name for you."

From toe to head, I assessed her. She wore black Nike sneakers, muddied in areas and mostly worn from the terrain, ripped blue jeans, a beige blouse with three Abalone buttons— two of which were unbuttoned, exposing a bit of cleavage. She couldn't have been more than fifteen, her dark eyes bright with hope. She had perfect bone structure and such a beautiful smile, which she was doing as I made my assessment. She was embarrassed at such scrutiny.

"Be nice to me," she joked, "or I'll make my own assessment of you."

"You, my dear, have no faults. Me, on the other hand, well, we won't talk about me."

"So, what is my name to be?" she asked eagerly.

"Veronica," I said definitively.

Her smile faded as she pondered it for a moment. "I love it. What does it mean?"

"Honey," I scoffed gently, "I have no idea. We Americans don't put much stock into such things. They are just names. Well, I suppose there is, of course, a meaning to most names, but we don't pay much attention. It is a shame, really. That's why I like it here. Everything has meaning... everything has a history."

"Either way, I like it very much. And when I go, I will use it."

It was getting late and the kids said their goodbyes. Malaika again gently brushed her new friend, "Veronica," and then the youngsters walked back to the main village.

Malaika stayed with me that evening, which was odd, but it did happen from time to time. She had something to tell me, but I couldn't quite pick it up. As I slept, I found her at my side in a dream, where the sky was baby blue with vanilla and soft magenta scraped across it. It was here she told me that Sanura was pregnant with a baby girl, warming my heart. As I woke, the sun was not yet up, but I could see the silhouette of Malaika's enormous head in front of me. I reached out sleepily. My hand caught her cheek, as I delicately rubbed her. She turned away slowly. I heard the screen slam shut as she made her way back into the night. Message delivered.

CHAPTER SEVEN

A bsko carried two bags of groceries at his side as he stepped onto the porch and into the kitchen area. I had been expecting him. As I loaded the groceries into the icebox, I pointed to his payment and asked him if he was going to tell his father, or if he wanted me to break the ice.

He was confused for a moment. "Tell him what?" he asked. "That I have a girlfriend? He knows."

I paused for a moment as I held a fresh cut of meat. "I know your secret."

"What secret?"

"The one you're keeping from your father. The one that you wanted to tell me, but I wouldn't let you." He slumped into himself, but then recovered, trying to deny with his body language that any such secret existed. "Sanura's pregnant," I said bluntly.

He caught himself by pressing his youthful hand against the wall. His dark face drained slightly at my news.

"How do you know? Did she tell you?" he gasped.

"No, Malaika stayed last night, and in a dream, she told me. That is why she only brushed against Sanura—fear of hurting the baby." Absko was blown away.

"Are you going to tell my father?" he panicked.

"No, not unless you want me to. Eventually he'll find out, of course. It's a matter of when. Absko, you are young, but I know you have a solid head on your shoulders. You're going to be fine. And Abasi might just surprise you."

He bit at his thumbnail at the thought of breaking the news to his dad.

"Do you have any names picked out? I was thinking Sherri."

"We're having a girl?!"

"My God, you don't know. Absko, I'm sorry. I should've known you didn't know yet. She's not even showing yet. I-I'm sorry I blew that."

"I'm having a girl!" he whispered delightfully under his breath. He stepped toward me, gleeful in the moment, picked me up, and hugged the living stink out of me as we bounced around in celebration.

"You going to tell your dad?" I asked.

"Not a chance. You tell him, but wait until he's had at least three lagers." Still beside himself with joy, he bolted for the door like a whirlwind as he ran back to the village.

"Where are you going?" I yelled.

"To Sanura! I have to tell her!"

A few days later, I found Abasi at my side. Two lagers down

and one more to go before I could spill it.

"Absko is tiptoeing around me. Do you know anything about this?" he asked me. I have not been known to keep secrets from him.

"Drink the third lager, and I'll tell you anything you want to know."

"Oh, that bad, huh?" he sighed.

"Depends on what you think is bad, I suppose."

"It's Sanura, huh?"

"Yep." I didn't hesitate. He probably just wanted to hear me say it.

"My friend," I said proudly, "you're going to be a grandfather."

"I know," he said sternly. Then he chucked his half beer into the field in a moment of aggression. "I wanted him to go to the university, and become something other than a tobacco farmer's son."

"Abasi, have you asked your boy what he wants for his life?" His blood boiled under his skin a moment longer, but as my question seeped in, he calmed down, shook his head, and told me he only wanted what was best. "Of course, every father wants that for his children."

We sat in silence for a while, then he opened another lager, sipped it, and sighed.

Shortly, his white teeth showed in a grin and he belted out a hysterical laugh. "My boy is his father's son. I was about his age when I became entangled in this exact scenario!" He reflected on the similarities. "Do Sanura's parents know?"

"I don't believe so," I said.

Abasi had to hold his belly as he doubled over in laughter. "Oh, I do not envy him. I have been there, and I do not envy him!" He began to brush tears of hilarity from his eyes.

"I think he is going to name her Sherri . . ."

He stopped laughing and turned to me. He then held his hands to his face, and began to weep.

"They're having a girl? I'm going to be a grandfather to a baby girl?"

I just let him be. In a moment, he had gone from the highest high to the deepest sorrow, only to end up in awe.

"You know university is not out of the question. He is smart enough. If he fully desired to accomplish such a feat, he could do it." Abasi felt I was placating him.

"Not with a little girl to raise," he countered. "Getting out of here is hard enough without a family."

"Not so. They don't call it America, the land of opportunity, for nothing. I could pull a few strings, find some grants and whatnot. When the time is right, and if he wants it, I could probably get him a long way."

"What about the baby and Sanura?"

"They could go too. Sanura has dreamed of going to America. Abasi, don't give up on your dreams for Absko. If they are his as well, there is always a way."

"Today we drink," he said. "Today my boy is a man. A budding man, but a man nonetheless."

CHAPTER EIGHT

At the meadow The Three stood stronger, taller than ever before. Malaika's body language was uncertain in a way I had not seen before. As they met her, she tried to pass, but the patriarch swatted her across the snout. She yelped in submission, and the females hissed while contouring their bodies into a pouncing stance. Instinctively, I stepped back in fear and then took one step forward, as if I could help. . . but I stopped. There was nothing I could do. She tried to pass through them again. A roar bellowed from the male's belly. Malaika gave up and withdrew. She turned toward me with sadness and then moved adjacent from her kin, seemingly no longer welcome in her pride, and passed through a different path down the ravine. The others traversed back the way they had come.

Change for the worst had come. Malaika had been staying with me for days at a time now. Her coat was becoming unkempt, and her mental stability had obviously waned. I learned that she was hunting solely for herself—now that she had been ostracized from her family. Although she could hunt, her confidence was failing her, for when she'd nab a kill, her cousins would be on her heels and would fight her for the kill. Most times she'd only get a scrap, and sometimes, not even that, depending on the mood of her kinship that day. Weeks passed and her deterioration continued. Fresh wounds accumulated on her face from continual defense of meals. It was becoming increasingly easy for her family to fend her off. Without proper meals, it seemed her joints began to ache, as her body became more and more emaciated.

I had asked Absko and Sanura to leave me alone for a while. They understood and relayed the message to Abasi. Only on occasion would they bring supplies, for which I was grateful. Of course, no one from the village came to assist my lioness friend. As we hunkered down for sleep one night, I tried one more time to feed her a cut of beef. I had tried several times over the past weeks. . . to no avail. I was relieved at what I saw next, but also deeply saddened. For this was the moment I knew she had truly lost everything, even herself. She was rolled up within herself, lying on a circle rug just off my bed. As I placed the cut of beef under her nose, she sniffed it as she usually did, and in one sorrowful moment, she opened her mouth and a discolored, infirm tongue rolled out and scraped the beef. She wept silently in her feline way—unseen, yet felt. She wept at my charity and for how far she had fallen.

I wept too. I didn't know what else to do. Soon after, we

both slept. In my dreams, she came to me.

"I am dying," she told me, as we walked through a familiar golden field. She continued, "I have been cut off from my family. What I speak of is not something you are familiar with. As I can communicate with you now, I had been able to do with my kin. Only now, I have been forbidden such spiritual connection with them. I no longer have it. It is a balance within my kind. One cannot live long without it. It is a source of life that all of my kind feed from. I cannot bear the silence. I hear nothing from them. It is as though I am blindfolded. My young are so distant. I cannot sense them. I have never had such feelings of hopelessness. I am not allowed to come near them or smell them, touch them." This was news to me. I hadn't realized she was a mother. But as I thought about it, of course, she would be. "I know why I have been shunned," she continued. "They tell me that our worlds cannot blend, as I know yours had told you. But they are wrong—we know this to be true. But their ways are ancient and solid. Much like yours."

I woke up to her voice still in my mind. "I'm alone," she said, as I caught her silhouette in front of me. I wept, still lying in bed as I reached for her. She turned before I could feel her coat. Even in the limited light, I could see her handicapped body as she hobbled away from me and through the front door.

The screen slapping the frame like a cat o' nine tails against innocent flesh.

I feared that night was going to be the last time I would see her. Like this was our goodbye. Luckily, it was not so. We spent many more months together. Even without the spiritual connection her soul yearned for, she was getting by, somehow. She was far from optimum indeed but she had recovered from her hopeless depth to a livable scenario. Mostly, I provided for her, and she stayed within the meadow's edges, with me. She wouldn't admit it, but she was frightened to go beyond the meadow. I was too.

Absko and Sanura—who was now many months pregnant—were used to Malaika. Although Absko and the cat did not wrestle anymore, occasionally, she'd throw in a head-butt or two to keep him on his toes.

One morning in June, while I sat in my chair, rolling my tobacco, sifting out stems as usual, Malaika's head snapped up and she turned her ears toward the meadow. She trotted as quickly as her legs would allow. She wasn't much for running, for she did not have the strength. At the meadow's edge stood The Three. I quickly made my way to our old exchange spot and found them all affectionately rubbing each other's coats and sniffing each other's faces. When she gazed back at me, I could see that glint again. That life! Her link was no longer severed. It appeared her sentence had been fulfilled.

CHAPTER NINE

bsko had been coming over more often. I got the feeling it was mainly for my benefit, rather than his. I hadn't seen Malaika since she had gone back to her pride, a good two months ago. I'd stopped putting out the coconut milk. I was frustrated and hurt, but past my selfishness I saw and understood the hell she had gone through. Why would she want to come back? I just wished she'd at least visit me in my dreams. Even this was out of bounds apparently.

I handed Absko a beer. He had graduated to this level of late. If you're old enough to have a baby, you can handle a beer. It helped that his father didn't seem to mind.

"I have a concern," he stated abruptly. I only looked at him, expectantly. "Sanura is very pregnant, and in about a month, she will give birth to our child." His voice was becoming thick. Whatever he had to say, it was something he had not discussed with his father. I had become adept at telling when he was confiding in me and me alone. "I am worried . . ." he said quietly.

"You are worried that what happened to your mother will happen to Sanura?" I asked compassionately. He sighed and nodded as he sipped. "Well, Absko, that is a concern, but an unlikely one. The hospital is a few miles away, and I believe it has French doctors. This is something your mother did not have access to, and medicine has come far since you were born.

I would not fear such an improbable occurrence. Just enjoy your wife and family. I think you'll be fine."

"What about you? Are you going to be fine?" It had been a long time since someone had asked me that.

"I'll survive." After a moment, we dropped this line of conversation and gazed upon the 'geti. "Have you thought about my offer?"

"University?" he asked.

"Yes, have you made any decisions?"

"Yes, in two years, I will take you up on your offer. I want to take Sanura and Sherri to America."

"That's good, Absko. I will do everything I can to make sure you have a good start. Don't be upset if I don't come along. I have a feeling I'll be here a while."

CHAPTER TEN

Like a portal to another universe, I found myself dreaming for the first time in months. And there she was. Malaika was at a distance, looking right at me. Happy. Her coat had recovered, and her body was strong.

"Come back," I asked.

"I'm far away," she said. It felt far to me.

"Will you come back?" I asked again.

She hesitated a moment. "Not likely. I am too far away," she said, and then turned away into nothingness.

When I woke the next morning, I felt recharged. I was elated to have heard from her. I knew that she was fine.

Another week had gone by and I still hadn't seen her. She doubted that she could come, and I understood.

One day I was with Absko at the tobacco fields.

"You got that all right?" I asked. He looked at me like I was an idiot as he wrapped up a bundle of last season's tobacco for me. As usual, he was shirtless—and ever more so had grown into a man. His baby was expected any day, and it showed; with his bright smile shining wherever he walked. He was as big, if not bigger than some of the men around him—most of whom were adjacent to us as they took a break from the fields. Banter and friendly insults flew around, most not understood by me.

I walked to a cooler about thirty feet away from him as he

finished up the bundle. As I lifted the lid, I felt a familiar bump against my leg. Malaika was radiant, joyful, and sweetly beautiful with her golden self, beaming with affection. I hugged her and rubbed her side. Just as Absko was about to raise the bundle, he caught her eye. Playfully, she hunched down into her pouncing stance and launched toward him. He was nearly ready for her when she tackled him to the ground. It happened so fast. In hindsight, I can't figure out why I didn't think this wouldn't happen. Of course, it would happen.

The men on their break, seeing a jungle cat on top of a boy would react in no other way. As Absko fell to the ground, although clearly laughing, these men, unaccustomed to the subtleties of pretended aggression, grabbed their machetes. Raising them high above their heads, they began running toward the boy.

I couldn't move my feet fast enough as I shouted to the men, "She's just playing!" I shouted it again and again. The first blow hit her flank. Yelping in pain, she rolled off Absko. Fearing for her life, she prepared a formidable defensive stance against the continuing onslaught. But there were just too many men coming down on her. With each blow and slash she writhed, her body wavering, bewildered by the blades buffeting down on her.

"NOOOOO!!" Absko yelled, but the mob could not be stopped.

"She's playing!" I implored at the back of the mob, desperately peeling them off as I made my way to her. I weeded through them until I finally held her. With Absko at my side, the mob begged off, giving us space. Most were cheering. . . I wept. Her body had been mangled. Pierced so many times. Her blood stained my hands as I looked into her eyes. She was alive, barely. Her tongue hung out as she weakly panted, blood filling her lungs. I wailed in my grief, and a few in the mob felt my loss, too. I could hear Absko explain that she was only playing. She was only playing. Most didn't care.

I felt a familiar hand upon my shoulder. As I turned, peering through tearful eyes, I found Abasi, mellowed and mournful. In his other hand was a pistol. I shrunk into myself, wailing "NO!" as I held her closer.

"My friend," Abasi whispered to me, "it is time. You must help her pass. Stop her suffering." I felt him slide the cold metal into my palm as he helped me to my feet. Reluctantly, I stood above her and in her agony she stared at me.

"Why?" I heard her say in my mind.

"I am sorry, Angel."

BANG!

She slumped as her body released the pain of the world. I collapsed to my knees while Abasi retrieved the pistol from my grip.

CHAPTER ELEVEN

A basi told me that Sanura had her baby, and Absko was filling the shoes of fatherhood nicely. I hadn't seen them in some weeks. I'd asked them not to come. My supply of coconut milk was gone. I couldn't stand the sight or smell of it anymore. I blamed myself. I had asked her to come back. This I'd never be able to get over. If it weren't for Abasi bringing me supplies, I'm not sure I could have endured the demons circling in my head.

As I sat with Abasi one evening, I asked him why he gave me the pistol. Why he didn't just do it himself. Why did I have to endure such a betrayal against a friend?

"Because if I had done it," he said, "you might never have forgiven me. And if a farmer had done it, it would have seemed like murder. Only a true friend would have compassion enough to put another friend out of their terminal misery."

I thought about that for a moment, not fully understanding, but at least I understood his intention in handing me the pistol.

"I must apologize to you." I turned to look at him, wondering what he had to apologize for. "I mistook her for a demon—for the demons that have killed members of my family—but it would appear you were right. She was an angel, and we—man—were the demon."

That evening I heard a cry beyond my meadow. It was the cry of the patriarch. I recognized his roar. As the sun met the horizon, I trekked to the perimeter of the meadow and beyond from where I stood, just ten feet away, were The Three. I felt completely vulnerable. I fell to my knees and sobbed. They held their composure, staunch and strong, as they witnessed this weaker species before them. As I looked into their eyes, I felt their loss. I hoped they could feel mine, for I truly repented the trouble I had caused. In the pit of my stomach I knew they knew what had happened, the moment it occurred. Their spiritual connection with Malaika must have been ripped from their collective consciousness, never to hear from her again.

The magnificent beasts rose to their feet in unison. The females left with their heads tilted down, but the king remained. He moved one step closer. I opened. . . I would not resist. He raised his head toward me in disdain. He then turned slowly and caught up to the females. I hadn't noticed before, but there were several other lions among them—all youngsters. I assumed they were Malaika's offspring.

One after another I received a stone-faced expression until all left me to wallow, alone.

CHAPTER TWELVE

I sagged in my chair, cigarette in hand. I relaxed and stared into the birthing sun as it rolled into the sky. I don't recall closing my eyes, but I must have, as the sky had transformed into a baby blue hue, scraped with gentle pastel fuchsia clouds. I stood in a breezy golden meadow as I have before with the high wheat tickling my palms. A jungle appeared before me where a golden light came to life from nothing. It was Malaika, showered in blissful light. Her nostrils poked at the air as she sniffed for tobacco smoke and coffee. I waved at her as her eyes deadened on mine and then softened. She turned slowly, knowingly. Her powerful hind legs gently negotiating the landscape as jungle shadows dappled her coat. I blinked, and she was gone.

My hand met my side. I didn't think she'd have anything to say to me after . . . then I heard it.

"Hi, Thomas!" rang in my mind. "I know—I'm better now—and Thomas . . . I *forgive you*. It is time you forgave yourself. Go, my friend. Your family needs you," she said, plain as day. No aggression, no sadness, no regret, no shame, just Love, just Understanding, and most importantly and heart wrenchingly painful for me . . . *Forgiveness.*

Maybe it was time for me to go home and do the same.

A Preview of Dreams of Eli

If you enjoyed MALAIKA, you may also like DREAMS OF ELI.

May 1863
Eli Age 26

During a skirmish two days ago, while in retreat, I lost my company. Somewhere in the backwoods of Northern Mississippi I finish a piece of stale bread, stand up, and lay my rifle against my shoulder.

It is not the crack of the enemy Enfield rifle round that startles me. It is the sifting whispers of the bullet as it splits the wild grass in my direction. The shooter, by the sound of it, is between four hundred and five hundred yards off. I know this because I have the same standard issue. The ball strikes me hard in the lower left shin. White searing pain shreds up my leg and body like a thunderbolt.

I stumble. My rifle catches most of my weight as I plow it into the soft earth from where I had just risen. But the shock is too great. I lose my grip—falling hard and fast to the cool soil where I crush my face against a large granite boulder. The flavors of shattered teeth and metallic blood sour my mouth. But all I can think about is the next eighteen seconds—enough time for my enemy to reload. The shot that I will never hear is upon me. I knew I would die in these woods. I just did not realize I would be alone. But at this end I do not want my brothers next to me. I want Cora. I wait for the final shot, but it never comes. Instead, blackness takes me.

CHAPTER ONE

May 1863
Eli Age 26

I hear nothing but ringing in my head. My legs and rump scrape against the ground at half a trot. A man is dragging me—to where I do not know. Feebly, I mumble something. My captor slows for a moment. He crouches over me for a listen, and then continues on. The daylight is unbearably heavy as my eyelids collapse. I fall back into oblivion.

April 1846
Eli Age 9

The first time I see her I am fishing with Ezra, an orphan Negro boy that is my best friend. I will never forget the moment I hear that twig break—those eyes. We both turn. Ezra says that he saw her first. To this day I do not know if he is right, but I do know I am forever changed. She comes out from behind a magnolia tree. I think she has been there awhile. We both stand as she bashfully makes her way down the hill to the edge of the water where our poles lay on the bank.

"You are that Negro boy-doctor, are you not?" she says, pointing to Ezra.

"I suppose I am. Ezra Johnson," he says, extending his hand. Ezra had been adopted by Mister Johnson, the town physician. He became the doctor's apprentice nearly two years ago. Already he is adept at bloodletting, lancing, and various herbal fever-breaking concoctions.

"You boys ready for a swim?" We are, however, she is not, seemingly. She wears a tattered off-white Sunday dress with no shoes. Before I know it though, both her bashfulness and her dress flop to the sand and a splash douses our faces. "Come on, the water is wonderful!" I have never swum with a girl before. I mean, not with one wearing only her unmentionables. For a nine-year-old boy I do not know what to do with myself.

Ezra stays at the bank. He never has liked to swim beyond the shallows. I have yet to ride him about this. I think it may have something to do with his parents.

"How come you have not asked my name?" I query, as I swim to her.

She smiles and spits water in my face. She laughs, "Because I already know your name. I know all about you, Eli." I am puzzled. "I know that you were born here and that you fish every Sunday."

"Really? What else do you know?"

"That you have been looking for a girl like me."

I blush. "How is that?"

"Word around town is you need help with the numbers. And I have been looking for something too."

"Really? What?"

"A boy like you . . . you know, a challenge."

"She rightly has you pegged, Eli," Ezra concedes.

"Are you some kind of math genius?" I ask.

She presses her lips into a wry smile. I am not sure how to respond to this, but I like it. As she swims away from me, her legs brush against me. A rush of something too good not to be a sin flutters through me. I am not totally sure what it is, but I know it came from her, and I want as much of it as possible.

She is not shy as she pulls herself from the water and onto the bank. Her bottoms are sheer and the water races down her slim body. I should turn away, but I cannot. So I stare at her as she slips her dress on, fighting with it as it sticks against her shimmering skin.

"I will see you, Eli." Her eyes reflect the blue sky. I gaze toward her, besotted.

"Wait!" I say. "When will I see you? What is your name?"

She giggles as she delicately negotiates the hill and turns back to me.

"Tonight is lesson one. My name is Cora. Cora Samantha Hannah." She disappears into the trees.

"Ezra," I say, "never in my life have I wanted to learn arithmetic more than in this moment."

Learn more about **Dreams of Eli** at

www.vanheerlingbooks.com

Made in the USA
Middletown, DE
03 October 2022

F

g

N
sc

co